FINGER PLAYS

MARIANNE YAMAGUCHI

Holt, Rinehart and Winston   New York   Chicago   San Francisco

For Kara

Here's a ball for baby

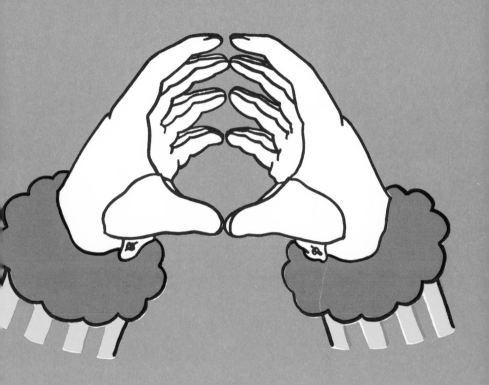

Big and soft and round!

Here is baby's hammer—

Oh, how he can pound!

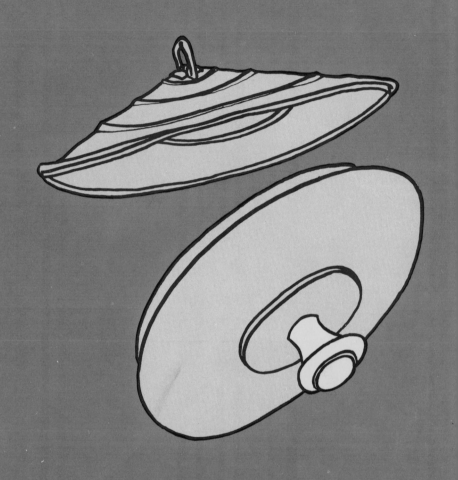

Here is baby's music,

Clapping, clapping so!

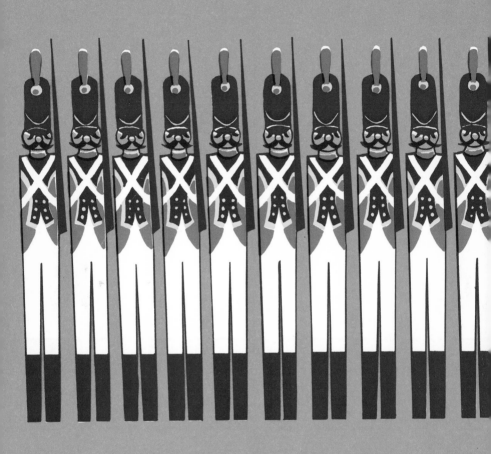

Here are baby's soldiers,

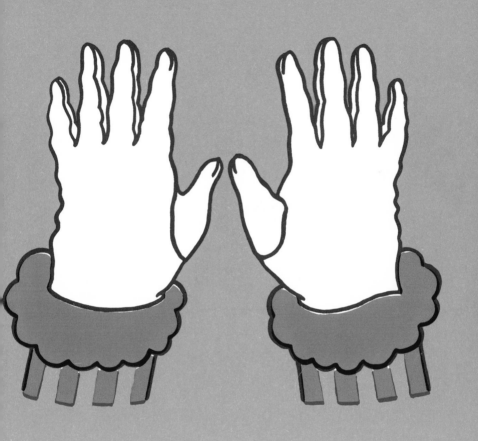

Standing in a row!

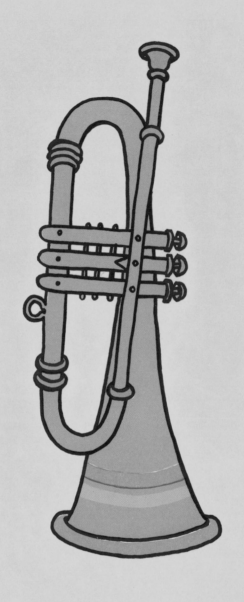

Here is baby's trumpet,

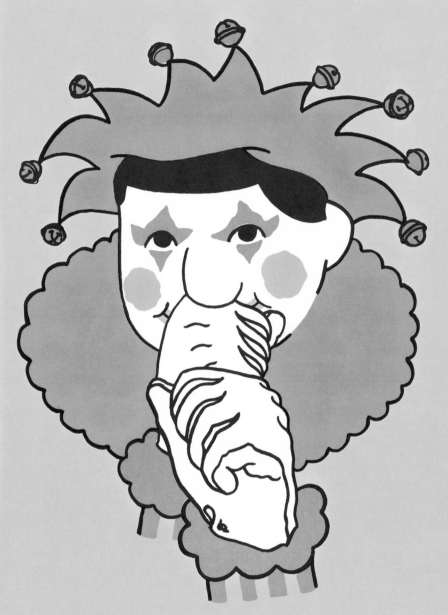

Toot-toot-toot! Too-too!

Here's the way that baby

Plays at "Peek-a-boo!"

Here's a big umbrella—

Keeping baby dry!

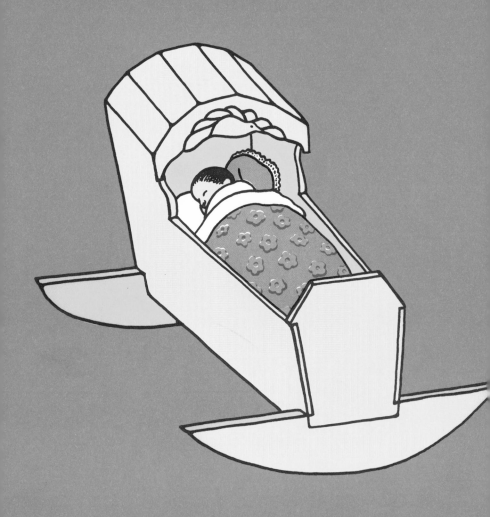

Here is baby's cradle—

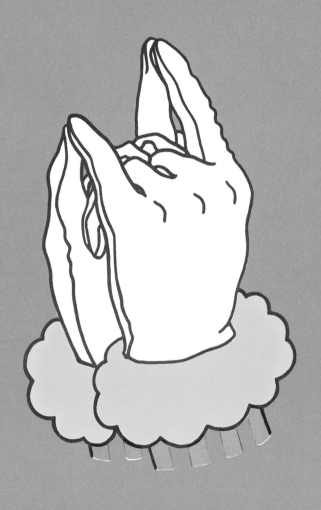

Rock-a-baby bye!

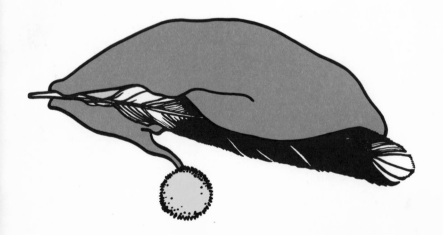

Two black magpies
sitting on a hill,

One named Jack—

The other named Jill.

Fly away, Jack!

Fly away, Jill!

Come back, Jack!

Come back, Jill!

This is the tree

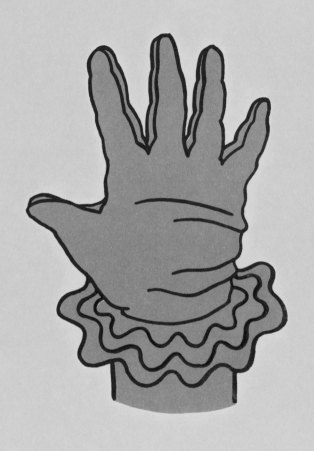

with leaves so green,

Here are the apples

that hang in between.

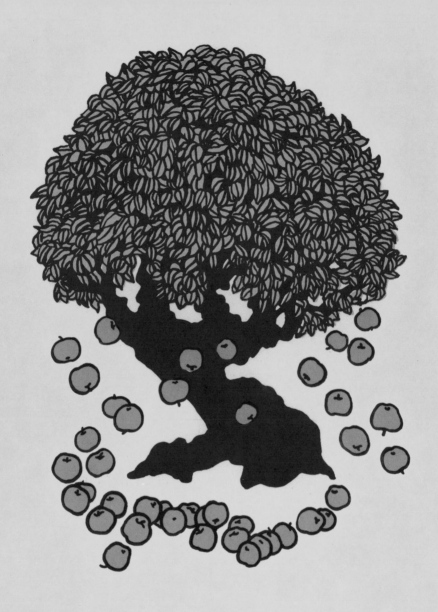

When the wind blows

the apples will fall,

Here is the basket

to gather them all.

ABOUT THE AUTHOR: Born near Cleveland, Ohio, Marianne Illenberger Yamaguchi graduated from the Rhode Island School of Design with a B.F.A. She began her professional career by illustrating two of her husband's books for children, *The Golden Crane* and *Two Crabs and the Moonlight*. Mrs. Yamaguchi wrote and illustrated *Finger Plays* "for very young children to follow by themselves, making their own discoveries through familiar objects." The Yamaguchis and their daughters, Esme and Kara, now live in Australia.

ABOUT THE BOOK: Mrs. Yamaguchi prepared the separations of the art on acetate, "against the window when the sun was bright and the windows clean." The display type is hand-lettered by the artist and the text typeface is set in photo Claro. The book is printed by offset.

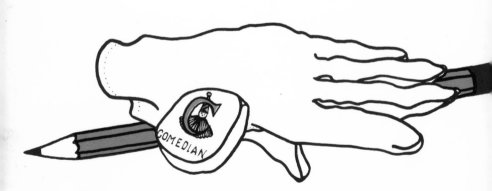